THE NILE FILES

Stories about Ancient Egypt

by Philip Wooderson

Illustrations by Andy Hammond

W
FRANKLIN WATTS
LONDON • SYDNEY

First published in 2001 by Franklin Watts
96 Leonard Street, London EC2A 4XD

Editor: Lesley Bilton
Designer: Jason Anscomb
Consultant: Dr Anne Millard, BA Hons, Dip Ed, PhD

A CIP catalogue record for this book is available from the British Library

ISBN 0 7496 3987 3 (hbk)
0 7496 4021 9 (pbk)

Dewey Classification 932

Printed in Great Britain

CONTENTS

INVITATION

Lord Lumpit regretfully requests your presence on the occasion of a solemn feast to be held in memory of his recently departed, dearly-beloved father, Troop Overseer Plonkitunbumpit.

R.S.V.P. Lord Lumpit
The Palace of Lumpit
Lumpit-by-Thebes

P. S. There will be dancing girls.

CHAPTER 1
DAD'S HIGH HOPES

Ptoni was very worried.

Dad had only got one thing to trade – a sphinx with a chip on its shoulder. And this was so large and heavy, it made their boat, *Hefijuti*, wallow and pitch. Even the smallest wave threatened to sink them.

But Dad was in high spirits.

"They don't make sphinxes like this any more! It was our lucky day when we took it from Blottumout. We could rent it out to some rich nob who'll pay me a regular income."

"But Dad, we don't know any rich nobs."

"I've been on the Nile long enough to know where to go to find nobles."

"Oh yeh. Where's that?" asked a crewman.

"Well . . . Kashpot could tell us," said Dad. "He's the richest, best-connected –"

"Crookedest –"

"Merchant in these parts."

They were passing Kashpot's palace – but there was no space to tie up *Hefijuti*. Alongside Kashpot's boat was an enormous galley, bristling with guards.

"Ah, Kashpot must have some rich guests!" Dad licked his lips. "In that case,

we'd better moor at the town quay. And I'll go and gatecrash the party while the lads are unloading the sphinx."

The lads didn't seem too keen.

Dad left them grumbling and groaning.

"Those lads of mine don't know how lucky they are. A healthy outdoor life, seeing the world, meeting people –"

"Look, Dad," said Ptoni. "There's Phixit!"

Phixit was Kashpot's Head Servant. He was hurrying out of the palace yard, waving his hands in the air.

"Ah, what a warm welcome," said Dad.

"Make yourselves scarce," shouted Phixit.

"Hey," said Dad. "Last time I was here, I saved you from being fed to the crocodiles, remember! Now go and tell your master that I've got a surprise for his guest. A sphinx!"

"I saw it," said Phixit, "on your boat. Thank goodness nobody else did. Our guest's an official from Thebes – on the track of a stolen sphinx!"

"No two are the same," said Dad, not in the least bit bothered.

"That's as may be," said Phixit. "But this official is giving a reward for information about any dodgy trader offering a precious sphinx dead-cheap. Of course, we don't know anything. Master never takes stolen goods."

Dad looked a bit disappointed. "Where else do you think we could trade it then?"

"Wherever you like," said Phixit. "But steer well clear of Thebes."

CHAPTER 2
MAKING AN OFFER

"That's a bit of a setback," said Dad. "Now where are those lazy lads?"

They found the lads with the sphinx. They were striking muscular poses outside Widow Wignite's Warehouse. The sphinx had a wig on its head, and a crowd was starting to gather.

"Just trying to flog your old sphinx, chief."

"All the best wig shops use sphinxes to display their wares."

"What rubbish!" Dad snatched the wig from the sphinx's head. "Do you really think that Widow Wignite could run to something this grand?"

"Depends on the terms." Widow Wignite glided out of her doorway in a waft of perfume and confronted Dad. "I'll offer you twelve of my prime plaited Nubian wigs in exchange for that crummy sphinx. Then you won't have to force your poor men to lift it ever again."

The lads looked pleased.

"Let's do that, chief. And we could trade her wigs in the market. That way you can settle our wages."

"You must be mad," exclaimed Dad. "A sphinx is a thing of great beauty, meant to enhance a gentleman's garden. It's not going to end its days outside a rip-off wig stall."

"But Dad," Ptoni tugged at his arm, "we can't keep on lugging it around. Try asking for twenty wigs."

Dad didn't seem to be listening. His eyes had gone strangely dreamy. Then he suddenly grinned. "Hello girls!"

Ptoni swung round.

Three shapely girls had just come out of the warehouse, wearing the latest plaited wigs.

"I'm Koy!"

"I'm Flirti!"

"I'm Brazen!"

"And I'm a top trader," blathered Dad. "I have my own ship . . . and these crewmen . . . as well as this priceless sphinx."

"It's beautiful."

"And so big, too."

"I bet it's worth a small fortune."

Dad nodded, well-pleased. "You can say that again. All I need to do is find a rich noble who wants to buy it."

Flirti fluttered her eyelashes. "Ooh, we know some very rich nobles."

"You do?"

Brazen walked up to Dad and looked deep into his eyes. "In fact, we've just been invited to an exclusive party – a funeral feast – at one of the grandest palaces."*

"But we're going to miss it," said Koy.

* Find out more about funeral feasts on page 60

"Why, what's the problem?" gulped Dad.
"We can't find a boatman to take us."
The lads rushed forward eagerly.

Dad held up his hand. "We're going that way, aren't we Ptoni?"

"Which way?" Ptoni asked.

Dad shrugged. "Whichever way these delightful ladies are heading."

Brazen took Dad's right hand and Flirti took his left hand.

And Koy just smiled.

"Thebes, you silly."

CHAPTER 3
NICE TO BE WANTED

Now Ptoni was twice as worried.

"Phixit warned us not to go to Thebes, Dad, and –"

"But he was just pulling our legs."

"Anyway, it's too far. We've got a stone sphinx on board – we can't manage the girls and their baggage as well. *Hefijuti* will sink!"

"Calm down, Ptoni. That stupid old tutor of yours, Stupor, has gone off to get some beer.

We can leave him behind – that'll keep the weight down."

So they left without Stupor. At least they thought they did. But as *Hefijuti* reached midstream, screaming broke out from the helm, where the girls were setting up camp.

"Help, it's a wild man," screamed Flirti.

"Save us," cried Brazen.

"Not just yet," screeched Koy. (She was still changing her robe.)

"Oh, drat it, that must be Stupor," growled Dad. Then, turning to the girls, he switched on a charming smile. "It's only my personal scribe. He's teaching Ptoni to read."

"He's been at the beer," whispered Ptoni as Stupor struggled to sit up, eyes bulging and lips wide open, showing his toothless gums.

"Bootiful boo –"

"That's enough. Time for a reading lesson," snapped Dad.

"And we've got to practise," said Flirti. "If you don't mind."

"Practise what?"

Brazen waggled her hips.

Ptoni suddenly understood. "You've been hired to *dance* at this party!"

Dad looked flustered. "Nice young girls like these wouldn't do that!"

"Why ever not?" said Flirti. "We dance at all the best parties."

"Go on," called the lads. "You show us –"

"Yes, give us a treat."

"Make our day!"

"Now, Ptoni," Dad was suddenly stern, "I said get over there with Stupor, behind the sphinx, and start learning."

Ptoni couldn't think what he would learn there, but Stupor said, "I were gwiff. Look at the thide of the thpinx!"

And sure enough there were hieroglyphs along the side of the sphinx. Ptoni went to look. But so did all three girls.

The deck started to tilt sideways.

"Don't all stay on that side," shouted Dad.

So everyone stumbled and staggered across to the opposite side, trying to balance the boat – just as a great gust of wind tugged at the sail. *Hefijuti* lurched over the other way.

The ropes that were holding the sphinx snapped.

The sphinx crashed onto its side.

And Stupor pitched into the Nile.

It took so long to fish Stupor out, and lash the sphinx down – on its side this time – that Dad had to give the order to moor for the night in the rushes.

The lads soon lit a fire, but there was nothing to cook except a small handful of beans. It wasn't a tasty feast.

Still, Stupor passed round his beer pot. "Dey thtill 'aven't done any darn thing."

"Darn what?" said Dad.

"Sing, thtoopid!"

"What me? I can't sing," said Dad alarmed.

"No!" the lads cried. "He means *dancing*. Come on, girls. *We'll* sing along!"

The lads started singing.

"*Row, row, row a boat,*
Gently down the stream,
Diddly-diddly-diddly-dote,
Life is but a dree-eee-eeeeeeeeeam."

Ptoni whispered to Dad. "Have you told those dancing girls how much you're going to charge for taking them down to Thebes?"

"It wouldn't be gentlemanly to charge them!"

"Why not? We've already run out of food."

"They'll help us some other way."

"How?"

"The sphinx can be part of their stage act. And then all the nobs at the party

will see it and want to own it. So they'll bid against one another, to try and impress the girls. The sky's the limit! We can't lose!!!"

Ptoni wasn't so sure.

And he was even more worried when they set sail the next morning, and saw lots of signs on the riverbank showing a large sphinx – with hieroglyphs underneath, including a drawing of something that looked like a cow shed.

"What does that say?" he asked Stupor.

"I fink it says WANTED," said Stupor.

"Isn't that great?" Dad said with a grin. "They must be desperate for sphinxes if they have to advertise for them!"

Ptoni had a sudden thought. He bent down and looked at their sphinx more carefully. Now that it was on its side he could see it was also marked on its base – with another hieroglyph which looked very like a cow shed.

But before he could make any comment, Brazen said, "Here we are! You want the next landing stage on the left. That big villa with the steps belongs to Lord Lumpit."

CHAPTER 4
A MINOR SETBACK

When Ptoni and Dad stepped ashore, Ptiddles decided to follow. But as they went further up the path, his tail got more and more bristly.

They carried on, passing an oblong pond with lots of big fish basking in it, through an archway, and into the kitchen yard. There were balls of dough on a table, baskets of vegetables and a jug of newly drawn wine. Ptoni could smell roasting meat.

"Is there anybody here?" called Dad. "Wake up, you lazy servants!"

"Who's that?" A man with big ears and three wobbly chins glared down from a window. "Clear out while you can, fools!"

"Rude oaf!" replied Dad. "I'll report you!"

"Who to? I'm Lord Lumpit!"

"Ah yes, of course." Dad was quick on the uptake. "Your Lordship, I bring you the finest dancing girls.* I've trained them myself specially for your party. They're known as the 'Sphinxy Minxes!'"

"I'm not going to have any party. The servants have all run away. Except for the cook. He got eaten."

"Who ate him?" gasped Dad.

"A lion."

* Find out more about dancing girls on page 61

Dad and Ptoni swapped glances. Then slowly they both turned their heads to look cautiously round the garden, only to catch sight of – Ptiddles! He was cowering under a stone bench.

"Perhaps you ought to c-c-catch it?"

"It's probably miles away now," Lord Lumpit said with a snort. "The question is – how did it get here? I bet my half-brother's behind this."

"Why? Didn't you invite him to the party?" Dad asked.

"I'd put on this feast specially for him! So we could make friends again. Not that I want to," said Lumpit, "anymore than he does. But it was our dear departed father's death wish."

Dad looked a bit more hopeful. "In that case, the feast must go on. In fact," Dad was cheery, "your troubles are over, Your Lordship. How lucky you are that we are here."

Lumpit stared at him blankly.

"Oh yes," Dad smirked. "I don't just supply the very best dancers in Egypt – I also have a son who knows how to train wild cats. He'll soon sort out a mere lion.* And we can do the catering too – moveable feasts to the nobs, sire – that's us. Just show us the way to your kitchens."

* Lions were prized animals in Egypt – see page 62

Ptoni whispered, "Who'll do the cooking?"

"The lads. You can help them," said Dad. "And Stupor can be the wine waiter."

"Dad!"

"Sssssh!"

"What will *you* do?"

"I'll have to look after the girls – make sure they're prepared for the show."

"The lads won't like this," said Ptoni.
"You'll be well rewarded," called Lumpit.

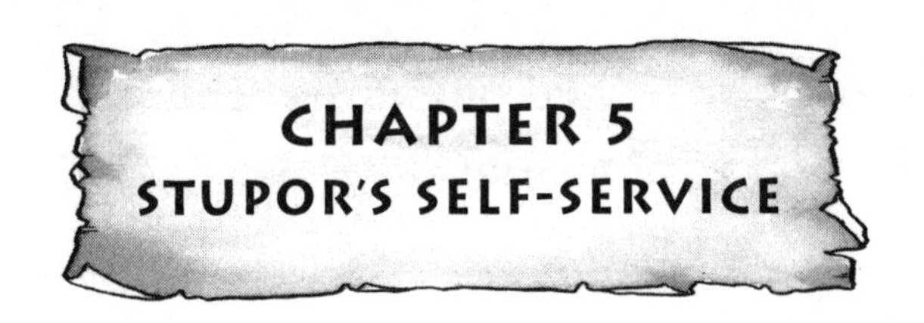

CHAPTER 5
STUPOR'S SELF-SERVICE

The idea of being rewarded made the lads ever so helpful. (Dad didn't mention the lion.)

"Oh yes. We'll do the cooking. We're pukka chefs, chief."

"No problem. Just leave things to us."

They even unloaded the sphinx without too many complaints, lugging it up the path and putting it down in the loggia overlooking the pool.

Then they helped put up some drapes, making a kind of closed stage where Dad said the girls could get changed.

The lads thought they could help there too.

"Go away and get cooking," said Dad.

This wasn't too much of a problem. A large cow was already roasting on a spit over the fire, so all they had to do was knead the dough into loaves and put them in the oven, while Ptoni chopped up the vegetables.

Time passed. The sun went down. The first guests arrived by boat, and Lumpit mooched into the kitchen.

He'd put on a princely robe, with princely jewels and a princely wig, but his big ears still stuck out, his chins were as wobbly as ever, and he still looked gloomy.

"Tell your butler to bring out the wine now. Lots of it. We're going to need it. You'll find more through there – in the closet."

The closet was cool and dark, and the air was heady with vapours wafting from giant wine jars. Then Ptoni heard Stupor's voice, sounding strangely muffled.

"Ethcape while oo can –"

Where was he? Trust Stupor to get at the wine!

"Lie on, thin ear –"

"Shut up, you old soak!"

Ptoni backed out, thinking Stupor was just talking nonsense. It was no good. He'd have to serve the wine himself!

CHAPTER 6
BROTHERLY LOVE

The guests were gathering round the pool as Ptoni handed them the goblets. But Lumpit stood by himself, looking grimly down the garden path towards the landing stage. A shiny galley had drawn up, manned by a beefy crew in colourful uniforms.

Trumpets blared as a man stepped ashore.

He wore an amazing plaited wig and lots of necklaces, and so many chunky rings his

fingers flashed in the lamplight. He had big ears like Lumpit, but otherwise he didn't look like his half-brother at all.

"Hi, Lumpit," he called, "still here then?"

"Yes, Sickup. Despite the lion you sent me this morning!"

"But that was a special gift!"

"A gift? It swallowed my cook!"

"Ah ha! That ought to pay you back for putting dead rats in my oil vats."

"I only did that because you sent some idiot to cut the heads off my prize plants."

"Come, nephews," said one of the older guests. "Remember you're brothers."

"No, Uncle Dunkit, we're *half*-brothers."

"Very well, Sickup, but all of us guests have come here to see you two make peace. It was your dear father's death wish."

"Huh! I was his favourite," said Sickup. "He could take Lumpit or leave him."

"No, *I* was his favourite," said Lumpit, "until he married your mother, and she sicked you up, and that spoilt things."

"Not for my father!"

"*My* father!!"

"If he hadn't married *my* mother, he'd only have had *your* mother. What an old crone!"

"How dare you! *My* mother was kind and generous, not like *your* selfish, stuck-up –"

"Stop this at once," cried old Dunkit.

"What do you think Pharaoh will say if he hears about all this squabbling?"

"You wouldn't tell him, Uncle Dunkit?"

"Well, Sickup, that all depends on whether we can settle down and enjoy a fine feast. Right, Lumpit?"

Lumpit snapped his fingers, and Ptoni raced back to the kitchen, intending to tell the lads to start dishing up the roast beef.

But they were out in the kitchen yard, lugging a hefty wine jar.

"Where are you off to?" cried Ptoni.

"We're taking our reward."

"You can't take it until after the feast!"

"There's not going to be any feast now. The food's already been gobbled up."

Ptoni looked at them blankly.

"By a big cat!" added one of the lads.

"Ptiddles?"

"Don't be stupid. This was a blooming great lion."

Ptoni felt cold all over as he heard Stupor's muffled voice replaying in his head.

"Lie on, thin ear –"

LION IN HERE!

"Oh no," gasped Ptoni. "Poor Stupor! He was in the closet."

"He's not any more," said one of the lads.

"We looked –"

"He must have been chewed up into little pieces."

As Ptoni looked at the lads in horror, they heard a loud noise from the kitchen.

"Don't let it out," yelled Ptoni to the startled lads. "Barricade it in the kitchen!" Then he rushed back to the garden to warn Lumpit – but he couldn't get a word in.

"You still owe me for the funeral. Fifty professional wailers don't come cheap," shouted Lumpit.

"I paid for the gifts to the gods. Bet they cost more!" shrieked Sickup.

"I paid for the mummification, all done by the poshest embalmers. Sukumout and Rappumup charged me an arm and a leg."

Ducking behind the curtain, Ptoni tried to tell Dad the news.

"Ptoni, look on the bright side," said Dad as he adjusted Flirti's skirt. "We can ask for an extra reward for capturing a lion like that."

"But there won't be a feast. There'll be trouble!"

"Nonsense. I'll start the show. There's nothing like dancing girls to take people's minds off their stomachs."

Then they both heard Sickup shouting. "I paid for the sphinx for his tomb! And I paid

to get it engraved. There was only a mark on its bottom before my masons got started."

"I don't think I saw the sphinx," said Uncle Dunkit.

"I'm not surprised. Someone swiped it. Probably Lumpit!" shouted Sickup.

"How dare you, you simpering weed!"

"Boggle-eyed toad!"

Dad rubbed his hands. "This is good for business. They'll want a replacement sphinx."

Ptoni thought of those Wanted posters all the way up the river. "But if this one looks like their old one –"

"All the better."

"No, Dad. Suppose it *is* their old one?"

"Relax, every sphinx is unique." Dad clicked his fingers as he pulled back the drape.

And the band struck up a bright tune.

CHAPTER 7
EVERY SPHINX IS UNIQUE

The Sphinxy Minxes came dancing out from behind the sphinx. They were wearing beads and black eye-paint, and hardly anything else.* Sickup's jaw dropped open.

"But that's my sphinx!" he gasped. "The one stolen from my father's tomb! Stop that racket at once!"

The musicians stopped. The girls stopped.

"Lumpit, you're a thief!" cried Sickup.

* Egyptians wore lots of make-up – see page 63

"No, he's not, sire," said Dad, strolling up to Sickup. "Lord Lumpit can't have taken this sphinx, because it belongs to me."

Sickup stared at him. "And where did you get it?"

"I took it from Blottumout's villa when I was doing a spot of tax collecting for Pharaoh. Blottumout hadn't paid his taxes."

Sickup narrowed his eyes. "You? Tax collecting for Pharaoh? Rubbish! I bet you stole my sphinx from my father's tomb and

sold it to Blottumout. And then pinched it back from him too. You're just a dodgy trader."

Dad's grin slipped right off his face.

But Brazen spoke up. "He's not dodgy. He's just not very bright. He thought you might like to buy it."

"Buy my own sphinx!" screeched Sickup drawing his sword. "Outrageous! I'm going to cut his head off!"

"Don't touch him!" Lumpit drew his own sword. "He's mucked up *my* feast. I'll do it!"

"Bu-but!" Dad was sweating, doing his best to keep jumping back out of the range of their swords. "Every sphinx is unique, sires. Just look at those hire-o-whatsits on the side."

"What do they prove," shouted Sickup.

Dad looked desperate. "Ptoni?"

All the guests crowded round, bending down to look at the hieroglyphs on the sphinx.

"It's somebody's name," said Ptoni.

"Whose name?" asked Uncle Dunkit.

"The sculptor's?" said Dad. "Or perhaps it just says 'Made in Egypt?'"

"It says Plonkitunbumpit," said Uncle Dunkit.

Sickup crowed. "That's my father."

"*My* father too," put in Lumpit.

"So that seems to prove it," sighed Uncle Dunkit. "But don't cut his head off near me, please. I've only just bought this robe."

Dad shot a wild look at Ptoni. "Why didn't you warn me about this. You just went on about sheds."

Ptoni was not looking hopeful. He turned back to Sickup. "Please, sire, if we'd known the sphinx had been stolen, we'd never have brought it back here. We saw all the Wanted signs."

"What Wanted signs?" asked Lumpit.

Uncle Dunkit chuckled quietly. "Oh I had those put up. You see, Chief Minister Donut has given me the job of tracing *another* lost sphinx. But that was a real antique – stolen from the tomb of King Milksop the Second. Pharaoh's offered a massive reward. He's desperate to catch the thieves. But, sadly, its only marking was something small on its bottom."

"Why, what's on its bottom?" said Dad.

"The seal of the House of Kouwshed."

Ptoni swallowed hard. "Does the seal look a bit like a . . . cow shed?"

"Uh, something like that. How did you guess?"

Ptoni took a deep breath, but before he could tell Uncle Dunkit, Lumpit honked like a

goose. "*Two* sphinxes, both missing. You're *sure* this one's yours, eh, Sickup? You didn't just 'find' it somewhere?"

"Wurgh, no. That is – I'm not so sure." Sickup was twisting his rings. "I might have made a mistake, though . . ."

"What sort of mistake?" said Dunkit.

"This one's got a chip on its shoulder.

didn't. I've changed my mind. It doesn't look like my sphinx at all."

"But it's got your father's name on!"

"It only says Plonkitunbumpit. I mean, lots of people are called that."

"Well, if it's not yours," said Lumpit, "I'll have it. I'll look on its bottom. And if there's a cow shed sign there, I'll claim the reward!"

"No, I found it first," exclaimed Sickup. "At least – no I didn't. Let's share it."

"It's worth making friends for," said Uncle Dunkit. "But you're going to have to shake hands and never quarrel again. And as for this ***very*** nice boy here," he nodded his head at Ptoni, "I think he deserves a reward too."

"What for?"

"For saving you," Dad said quickly. "He managed to catch that lion. It's safely secured in the kitchen." Dad beamed. "Good old Ptoni. He's a real wizard with lions. He loves them. He adores them. Much better than boring old sphinxes!"

Sickup put his sword down, so Lumpit did as well.

"Yes," Dad prompted, "I wonder what sort of reward?"

"Better give him the lion," said Lumpit.

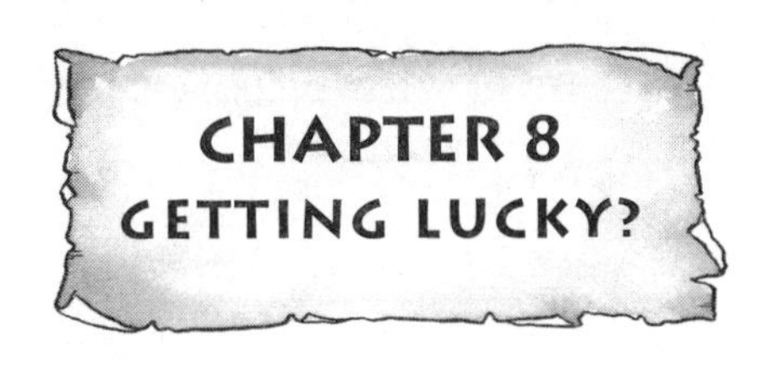

CHAPTER 8
GETTING LUCKY?

So *Hefijuti* sailed away with a large wooden cage on the deck, containing one angry lion.

And they were out in midstream before they saw the three girls waving frantically from back on the landing stage.

"Oh dear," said Dad. "We forgot them."

"They got us into that mess, Dad."

"No, Ptoni, it wasn't *their* fault."

"Oh, no? So whose fault was it?"

The lads were pointing at Dad.

"I hate speaking ill of the dead," said Dad. "But I have to say I blame Stupor. I mean, if he'd paid more attention to all those Wanted signs and the cow shed on that jinxed sphinx's bottom, we could have taken it back to the Temple at Thebes and claimed a proper reward. We might have been rich by now. But thanks to him, we've got nothing to trade but one mangy cat –"

"Grr!" said Ptiddles.

"Two mangy cats."

"*Grrrr*!! *Grrrr*!!"

"And nothing to eat," said Ptoni.

"We've got a large wine jar," said one of the lads.

"We managed to lug that on board. And I could just do with a drink!"

But when they opened the lid they had a nasty surprise.

"There's no wine in there!"

"It's empty."

"It isn't. There's something inside it."

Stupor popped his head out.

Nobody spoke for a long time.

Then Dad gave a hopeful chuckle. "Come on, lads. Look on the bright side."

"What bright side is that?"

"Tell us, chief!"

"Well . . ." Dad had to think for a while. "I mean. Well isn't it lucky that Stupor's still with us. It proves that our luck's started to change."

"Oh yeh?"

"And why should it do that then?"

"Becoth," Stupor gave them a toothless grin, "he's got wid of dat horrid jinxthed thpinx."

Funeral feasts

Egyptians believed in life after death. They went to great lengths to prepare themselves for death, burial and the life to come. Tombs were filled with objects that would make life comfortable – clothes, furniture and food.

After the burial ceremony, funeral guests held a large feast in honour of the Departed.

Dancing girls and musicians

Professional dancers and acrobats performed at feasts, festivals and marriages. They were accompanied by musicians who played such instruments as flutes, pipes, lutes and harps. Rattles, cymbals and drums beat out the rhythm for the dancers.

Lions

Lord Lumpit was fortunate to have been given a lion. They were rare animals in Ancient Egypt and were much prized.

Pharaoh Ramesses II possessed a pet lion, called "Tearer-to-Pieces-of-his-Enemies". This big cat used to run behind the Pharaoh's chariot when he went into battle.

Make-up

Both women and men wore make-up in Ancient Egypt. They used eyeliner called kohl, made from ground copper or iron ore and mixed with oil. Lips and cheeks were painted with red clay mixed with water. A dye called henna was used to redden nails and hair.

Wealthy men and women bathed often and had their bodies massaged with ointments, oils and perfume. Egyptian scents, made from flowers and fragrant woods, were famous throughout the Middle East

Join Ptoni and his Dad up the Nile
in these other books.

THE SCRUNCHY SCARAB

0 7496 3649 1 (Hbk) 0 7496 3653 X (Pbk)

The town of Feruka is having a big celebration, but all Dad has to sell are some dried-up figs and a few old flasks of oil. Fortunately Ptoni finds a lucky scarab beetle – so perhaps things will change for the better?

THE MISSING MUMMY

0 7496 3650 X (Hbk) 0 7496 3654 6 (Pbk)

Dad goes to collect some wine he is owed by Slosh, the merchant. But poor Slosh has died, and someone has stolen his mummy. It's up to Ptoni to find it, and to claim the wine.

THE FEARFUL PHARAOH

0 7496 3651 3 (Hbk) 0 7496 3655 6 (Pbk)

Pharaoh Armenlegup is having a big festival to celebrate his long reign. So everybody is happy – everybody, that is, except Dad. He's been sentenced to death!

THE HELPFUL HIEROGLYPH

0 7496 3652 1 (Hbk) 0 7496 3656 4 (Pbk)

Pharaoh has ordered Dad to pick up some taxes for him – but Dad can't read. So he hires an old scribe to teach Ptoni how to understand the hieroglyphs. It's a harder job than they thought!

THE POINTLESS PYRAMID

0 7496 3988 1 (Hbk) 0 7496 4022 7 (Pbk)

When three sinister-looking men ask for a lift, Dad is happy to oblige. But trouble breaks out even before they reach their destination – the spooky Pointless Pyramid!